Bailey
Goes Camping

By Kevin Henkes

SCHOLASTIC INC.

New York Toronto London Auckland Sydney
Mexico City New Delhi Hong Kong

FOR LAURA

ISBN 0-439-07373-1

12 11 10 9 8 7 6 5 4 3 2 1   9/9 0 1 2 3 4/0

Printed in the U.S.A.   23

First Scholastic printing, May 1999

Bruce and Betty were Bunny Scouts.

They were going camping.

Bailey had to stay home.

"I want to go camping," said Bailey.

"You're too little to go," said Bruce.

"But in a few years you can," said Betty.

"Don't feel bad, Bailey," said Bruce. "It's not *that* great. All we do is eat hot dogs and live in a tent and go swimming and fishing and hunt for bears and tell ghost stories and fall asleep under the stars."

"And don't forget roasting marshmallows," said Betty. "That's best of all!"

Bailey watched Bruce and Betty leave.

"It's not fair," he said.

"Come on," said Papa, "let's play baseball."

"No," said Bailey.

"Want to help me bake cookies?" said Mama.

"No," said Bailey.

"We could read a book," said Papa.

"No," said Bailey. "I want to go camping."

"You're too little to go," said Papa.

"But in a few years you can," said Mama.

"Don't feel bad, Bailey," said Papa. "It's not
that great."

"Oh, yes, it is," said Bailey. "You get to eat
hot dogs and live in a tent and go
swimming and fishing and hunt for
bears and tell ghost stories and fall asleep
under the stars. And best of all, you roast
marshmallows."

"You know," said Mama, "you can do
all those things right here."

"I *can*?" said Bailey.

"He *can*?" said Papa.

"Yes," said Mama, smiling.

That afternoon, Bailey ate hot dogs

and lived in a tent.

He went swimming

and fishing.

That night, Bailey went on a bear hunt

and told ghost stories.

And best of all,

he roasted marshmallows—

before falling asleep

under the stars.